Lenny & Puppy

The Adventurous Alpacas

Written by

Cindy Dittfield

AuthorHouse™
1663 Liberty Drive
Bloomington, IN 47403
www.authorhouse.com
Phone: 1 (800) 839-8640

Published by AuthorHouse 02/16/2019

ISBN: 978-1-5462-7993-8 (sc)
ISBN: 978-1-5462-7992-1 (e)

Library of Congress Control Number: 2019901630

Print information available on the last page.

This book is printed on acid-free paper.

authorHOUSE®

To Michael, my love for you grows with each adventure.

For my parents who gave me life lessons.

For my children, Mike and Morgan, who endure them with love.

Puppy was a young lonely alpaca who lived on a small animal farm in the country. It was a rural area with huge open spaces, warm sunshine and blue skies. There were acres and acres of farmland where the farmers grew corn and beautiful sunflowers. Along the road, you would pass farms with large barns where they raised chickens, goats and sheep, but on the farm where Puppy was born, there were different kinds of farm animals. He lived with other alpacas, a few llamas, and colorful birds called peacocks.

Puppy was still smaller and younger than most of the other alpacas on the farm. He had a dark heavy coat which alpacas call fiber. Puppy wasn't the cutest alpaca. His bangs were long and hid his eyes, and he was usually covered in bits of hay. He spent most of his time by himself, playing and grazing in the field.

Being the youngest on the farm, Puppy wanted to play and herd with the older alpacas, but they didn't have any interest in galloping along with him. They preferred to graze in the field. When he did become playful with them, they would quickly give him an alpaca warning nudge, and spit until he would stop his nonsense. They thought he was just a silly, young alpaca, but believe it or not, Puppy wasn't as young or silly as they thought.

You see, every morning at feeding time the farmer would take his bucket and give each alpaca some grain in their own bowls. The bowls were lined up in a row. Because the alpacas were hungry and always in a hurry to be fed, they would always leave their bowl and look in the next bowl as the farmer went down the line.

Puppy noticed their impatience, and being a pretty clever alpaca, he would stay back from the herd and wait. Once the older alpaca moved to the next bowl, he would step up, drop his head and eat up all the grain they left behind. The other alpaca didn't think Puppy could see very well because of his heavy bangs, but he could see just fine. He found his way to the full bowls every time.

But sadly, after feeding time, Puppy was left pretty much to himself. He was lonely and maybe even gloomy at times, but he had a sweet way about him and was always willing to snuggle up to a visitor with a handful of grain. He did hope for a playmate, and wished one would arrive in the trailer that sometimes brought new animals to the farm.

One day in the late summer, Puppy noticed activity on the other side of the fence where the lady alpacas lived. The farmer's wife was calling for help. Most times, Puppy really didn't pay much attention to the lady alpacas, but today was different. There was an energy in the air, and yet all the lady alpacas were standing around quietly. It was like they were waiting for something special to happen. But what?

He heard the farmer's wife on the phone yelling "a baby is on the way!" Was the trailer coming? Were new animals coming to the farm today? Puppy was certain this was going to be a big day.

There had been a bad storm the night before that knocked out the power and there wasn't any clean water available on the farm. The farmer's wife had called the neighbors, asking them to come quickly and bring any water they had.

"Have you got any power?" she asked.

"We need water! We've got a baby coming!!!" she yelled.

The next sound Puppy heard was familiar. It was the neighbor's 4-wheeler coming down the road to the gate. He immediately thought of breakfast, because these neighbors had helped the farmer feed him and the other animals when the farmer wasn't home.

These neighbors came to the country from the big city and didn't know much about farms or animals, but when asked to pitch in, they always said yes. They grew to love the alpacas, along with all the other animals on the farm, so when the farmer's wife called about a baby coming, they were very, very excited.

When they arrived, the baby alpaca had just come. It was a boy!

"He's so cute," the neighbor said.

"What happens now?" she asked.

"Well, now we wait for him to stand on his own and take milk from his mother," the farmer's wife replied.

They all watched and waited. Within a few moments, the little baby alpaca, a cria, tried to stand. His legs wobbled, but with each try he became stronger and stronger. A few minutes later he was up on all four legs and trying hard to walk. He took a few steps, found his momma and began to drink milk. According to the farmer's wife, this was a very good sign that he would be a healthy alpaca.

The neighbors immediately loved the little guy. The wife said, "What should we call him? He looks like a Lenny. Let's call him Lenny."

Her husband laughed at the odd name but quickly agreed that Lenny was a great name.

From the other side of the farm, Puppy saw Lenny being born and take his first steps. He was excited. There was a new little boy alpaca on the farm. Maybe it was a friend for him? He could only hope.

The neighbors came by often to see Lenny, who was housed in the cool barn with his momma during the hot summer days.

Lenny grew attached to them quickly. He began to love when they came to visit and started dancing and prancing around when he saw them or heard their 4-wheeler coming down to the farm.

As the months went by, Lenny began to change. His fiber was a light brown color and he was beginning to look fluffy like the rest of the herd. Lenny had big brown eyes and a mouth that always looked like he was smiling. He was soon let out of the barn and now spent his days hanging with his momma and the other lady alpacas in their field.

Puppy kept wishing that one day Lenny would be his friend. He often stood by the fence watching Lenny play with the ladies. He knew it would be a while before Lenny would be old enough to leave his momma and live on the boys' side of the fence with the other male alpacas.

When the fall came, the farmer and his wife were out in the field and Puppy overhead them talking.

"We need to thin out the herd," the farmer's wife said.

"Yes, we're getting older and it's going to be harder on us as time goes on. I think I know someone who would love to adopt some of these wonderful alpacas for their farm," the farmer replied.

"That's wonderful!" she replied. "We certainly want to be sure they are all with good folks and have wonderful places to live. But what about Lenny? He's still very young, and I'm not sure he should be adopted by just anyone."

"I don't know what would be best for our little guy, but we'll figure it out," replied the farmer as they walked away.

Puppy hung his head. I'm going to be adopted. He sighed.

On Christmas morning, the sun was bright in the sky. The farmer came out to the field to feed the alpacas and stopped at Puppy's bowl.

"Today's going to be a big day for you, little guy," he said.

Puppy had a belly ache and didn't even try to steal the older alpacas' grain that morning. He just didn't feel like eating. He didn't know what was going to happen to him and where he would be living. All he could think about was what he heard the farmer and his wife saying about being adopted.

After breakfast, Puppy heard the farmer's wife on the phone.

"Merry Christmas!" she said.

"Can y'all stop by today? We've got a gift for you."

Soon after that phone call, he heard the 4-wheeler. The neighbors were coming.

Lenny's ears also perked up when he heard the 4-wheeler. He had already learned the sound of the neighbors' arrival.

Then he heard the neighbor man yell. "Len. Hey Lenny! Merry Christmas!"

Lenny started jumping and prancing when he saw him. The neighbor held out his arms for a big Christmas hug and Lenny jumped right in.

Puppy felt his little alpaca mouth smile and his alpaca heart swell with love when he saw the hugs and special love. What about me? he thought.

Then he heard it. His wish came true.

"Merry Christmas, Puppy," the neighbor lady said.

Although Puppy had been on the farm awhile now and enjoyed the special attention, he couldn't help but be a little shy when she came over to him. She offered him some hay from her hand. He took a little nibble and quickly felt at ease.

"We have something for you," the farmer said as he handed the neighbors a card.

The neighbor lady opened the card and began to read aloud.

"The farmer and I would like to give you a special Christmas gift. You've been excellent friends and helpers....Lenny is yours. Merry Christmas!"

"If you'd like to have him," the farmer's wife added.

The neighbors were surprised by their wonderful gift and already loved the little alpaca so much they agreed immediately.

Everyone was so happy.

Then the farmer reminded them. "He'll need a companion because alpacas prefer to live with other alpacas."

The neighbors thought about it for a moment or two and said, "If you're okay with it, we'd like to take Puppy as his companion. He is sweet and they should get along very well."

"Perfect," they all agreed.

Puppy was beside himself. Not only was he being adopted, he was going to be adopted with the new alpaca, Lenny. They would be long-time friends, but where would they be going?

How will they get there? Puppy had so many questions.

By the time springtime came, Puppy noticed that Lenny was venturing away from the lady alpacas and becoming more interested in things going on over on his side of the fence. Longing for a special friend, Puppy always positioned himself close to where Lenny had been playing when one day, he suddenly heard someone whispering.

"Mrrr. Hi. I'm Lenny."

"Hi. My name is Puppy." He smiled.

"Will you be my friend, Puppy? I'm going to be moving over to the boys' side soon, and I don't know any of the boy alpacas."

"Sure, Lenny. That's awesome. I would love to be your friend, but there's something I have to tell you."

Lenny looked at Puppy with wide eyes. *What could he possibly have to tell me?* he thought.

"What is that Puppy?"

"You and I are going to be moving."

"What? Moving? Where?"

"Let me explain. The farmer and his wife gave us to the nice neighbors who come on the 4-wheeler and play with us. We are going to live with them."

"That's great news!" Lenny exclaimed.

Puppy was a little confused. How could Lenny be so excited about moving away from the big farm?

"When?" Lenny asked.

"I don't know, but soon I suspect."

The neighbors always came by to visit Lenny, and each time Puppy thought that was the day they would be moving. But most days they just helped the farmer or played with Lenny and went home. Puppy kept pacing along the fence, talking to Lenny about moving to the neighbors'. He couldn't stop worrying.

Lenny always encouraged Puppy with positive thoughts and words. "Don't worry, Puppy. It'll be okay."

It was the following summer when Lenny was fully grown that it was time to make the move. The farmer pulled the trailer into the field and loaded Lenny inside. He happily galloped along and stood in the trailer waiting patiently for Puppy.

When the farmer came to collect him, Puppy was afraid and ran away. But then he thought about his friend Lenny, loaded in the trailer, waiting for him. Puppy realized after a long time he finally found a friend. How silly it would be to let him go!

So, he slowed down and let the farmer catch him. Before Puppy knew it, the two of them were in the back of the trailer when their adventure began.

"I'm excited!" said Lenny.

"I'm a little frightened," Puppy replied.

Lenny turned to Puppy and smiled his little alpaca smile.

"You never have to worry as long as we're together. I'll always look out for you. You're my best friend, Puppy."

Puppy's heart swelled with love. He did have a best friend, and together they were about to experience a wonderful adventure.

Lightning Source UK Ltd.
Milton Keynes UK
UKHW051821260219
338072UK00007B/89/P